My Amazing Toddler
Behavioral Series

I Play Nicely.
I Am GENTLE!

By Suzanne T. Christian

TWO RAVENS
B O O K S

Two Little Ravens
CHILDREN'S NON-FICTION BOOKS

Paperback Edition: 9781964202112
Hardcover Edition: 9781964202129
Digital Edition: 9781964202136

Published in the United States by Two Ravens Books LLC,
254 Chapman Rd, Ste 209, Newark DE 19702

'Expand the mind, free the imagination, one title at a time.'
www.tworavensbooks.com

Welcome to
"I Play Nicely. I Am Gentle!"

This book is a charming collection of easy-to-understand affirmations created especially for young children. As you journey through its pages, your child will learn the value of gentleness, empathy, and kindness.

Each page showcases vibrant illustrations and relatable scenarios that promote loving and gentle interactions. Incorporating this book into your daily reading routine lets your toddler gradually embrace gentle behaviors, as repetition is a key to learning.

Get ready for a fun and meaningful experience with your little one!

Suzanne T. Christian

I am kind and gentle
every day.

Being gentle
makes me
a good friend.

I play nicely because it makes everyone happy.

My hugs are like
soft clouds.

Gentle hands,
gentle heart.

I use my gentle hands
to play with my toys.

I am gentle,
just like the wind.

I help others with
my gentle hands.

I am gentle,
just like my favorite
teddy bear.

When I see a ladybug,
I hold it gently.

My gentle touch
makes my pet happy.

I do not pull
my pet's tail.
I am gentle.

When I play with
my baby brother,
I'm always gentle.

When I feel angry,
I take a deep breath
and stay calm.

I wait my turn with
a happy smile.

I give gentle pats when someone is sad.

I gently put away my toys.
I do not throw them.

I play quietly when others are sleeping.

I gently knock on a door before entering

I can be gentle even
when I'm excited!

Gentle hands mean
happy playtime.

I play nicely.
I am gentle!
The End!

My Amazing Toddler Behavioral Series

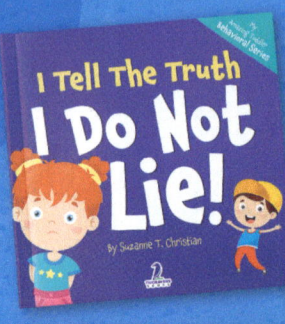

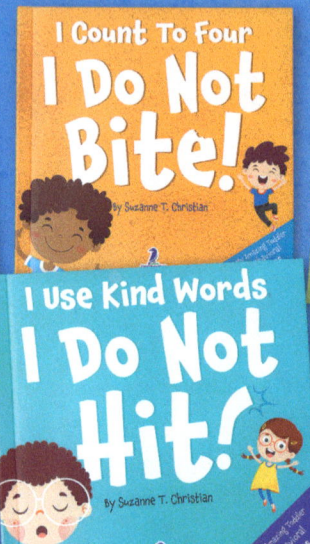

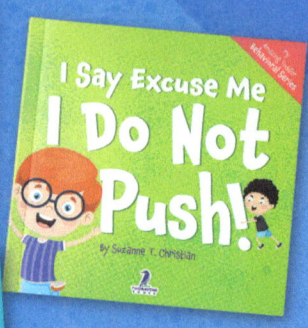

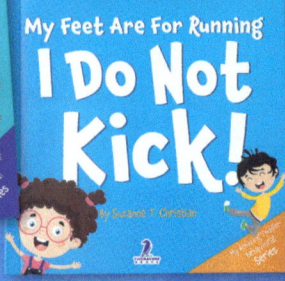

Check Out
Suzanne T. Christian's beloved series
'My Amazing Toddler Behavioral Series'.
Young readers are sure to enjoy!

Two Little Ravens
CHILDREN'S NON-FICTION BOOKS

Dear Amazing Reader,

Thank you for diving into **I Play Nicely. I Am Gentle!** with me. If this book touched your heart or made a difference for a young reader, I'd be grateful if you could share your thoughts in a review. Your feedback inspires my future work and helps others discover the magic within these pages.

I'd love to hear from you directly if you have suggestions or ideas for improving the book. Please feel free to reach out to me at **suzanne.christian@tworavensbooks.com.** Your voice counts, and I cherish it deeply.

With heartfelt gratitude,

www.ingramcontent.com/pod-product-compliance
Lightning Source LLC
Chambersburg PA
CBHW041559120626
46551CB00002B/265